I0630326

4 EASY Steps

To SWITCH From JOB To SUCCESSFUL ENTREPRENEURSHIP

Success Coach Nilesh

VISHWAKARMA
PUBLICATIONS VP ®

4 EASY Steps To SWITCH From JOB To Successful Entrepreneurship

First Edition - January 2017
© Author
This Life Changing Book is Proudly brought to you by

ISBN: 978-93-85665-44-8

Published by:
Vishwakarma Publications
283, Budhwar Peth, Near City Post, Pune- 411 002.
Phone No: (020) 20261157 / 24448989
Email: info@vpindia.co.in
Website: www.vpindia.co.in

Cover: Success Coach Nilesh and Team

Typeset and Layout: Chaitali Nachnekar (Vishwakarma Publications)

To my father, Dr. Manikrao Waghchoude,
for his
deep love, care, and trust in me

"Respect, recognition, and reward flow out of performance."

— Narayana Murthy

Success Coach Nilesh at Press event, 2014

" *If you don't build your dream, someone else will hire you to help them build theirs* "

— *Dhirubhai Ambani*

Congratulations

The Ability to do what you love is one of the most Powerful Skills. Many want it but very few get it. Being an expert in this arena will reap massive rewards. Therefore it is worth putting your time, money and resources in building your Successful Business. It not only gives you a sense of satisfaction but also brings a sense of purpose to your life.

Congratulations on starting this journey. I know it will change your life and the lives of those who will be touched by your business.

All the Best!

Yours Sincerely,
Success Coach Nilesh
www.SuccessCoachNilesh.com

" Risk more than others think is safe. Dream more than others think is practical. "

— Howard Schultz

Contents

Acknowledgments

As Helen Keller, the deaf-blind American Author, has said, "Life is either a daring adventure or nothing at all".

In my daring adventure, I am blessed to meet certain people who have helped me shape my life.

I would first like to thank my wife Meenal for patiently listening to my dreams and ambitions and for supporting my numerous attempts to make this book the best experience for you, the reader. She is one of my first audience.

I would also like to thank my sister, Neelima, my brother-in-law and friend Jeevan, my mother Sunita, and my brother Sanket for their love and care.

I would like to acknowledge and appreciate help from my colleague Rohini, whose efforts helped me put all this content together so that it can make sense and change lives.

Next, a huge thanks to my friends, clients and all the people who have helped me grow both personally and spiritually.

Special thanks to Vishal Soni and his team at Vishwakarma Publications who have helped me bring this book to you.

Everyone matters.

" *Perfection is not attainable, but if we chase perfection we can catch excellence.* "

—Vince Lombardi

Preface

Entrepreneurship is a vital source of change needed in the society. The general trend of the society has been that we encourage people to become doctors, engineers and so on. But very few help or assist others in the regards to becoming an Entrepreneur which is very unfortunate. Entrepreneurship empowers individuals to create multiple job opportunities; change lives and paves the path towards innovation and economic growth. Entrepreneurship gives Sense of Satisfaction, Freedom and Sense of Contribution to make this world a better place. One-third of the world's population is lacking access to basic energy and 71% of the world's population lives on less than $10 a day. In such scenarios, entrepreneurship can play a vital role in finding solutions to problems faced by human civilization. Our society or world, in general, is in need of individuals who have the courage and dream to bring about this much-needed change.

The journey of Entrepreneurship can seem lonely because you will be burning the midnight oil to look after various pieces of the unknown puzzle and it will seem like giving up in between. Imagine you are going on a mountain climbing adventure. It's all excitement and passion at the beginning. However, when the terrain gets harder you may feel like stuck somewhere in between. You can't even go forward due to obstacles and you can't even return due to fear of failure or what other people will say about you. To help you successfully handle all these emotions and to assist you in exploring the window of opportunities, a good book can be very useful. Many books have been written on entrepreneurship but this book will guide individuals who are seeking help to move from their regular 9 to 5 job to successful entrepreneurship. This book is easy to understand and has a step by step approach towards shifting from job to entrepreneurship. The illustrations provided in the book can help readers understand the steps much easily. The steps explained in the book are tried and tested and it has been made sure that all the risks are handled correctly before taking the big jump. In addition to that, this book has motivational quotes that will encourage the readers to pursue their dreams and fill their lives with positivity, new energy and hope.

This book is designed for individuals, who are currently in their job but have a dream to venture into entrepreneurship. The book can also be read by entrepreneurs who are facing obstacles and challenges in their entrepreneurial journey. No prerequisite knowledge of entrepreneurship is needed to understand this book. To take the maximum benefit of this book, the readers need to read this book multiple times, understand the concepts, take necessary actions mentioned at the end of each step and go ahead overcoming all fears. This book is a guaranteed guide towards entrepreneurial dream realization. If the readers diligently go by the steps mentioned in the book nobody can stop them from achieving their dream to become a successful entrepreneur and change the world into a better place.

> *Repetition makes reputation and reputation makes customers.*
>
> —Florence Nightingale Graham

WHEN YOU FAIL DON'T FIND
REASONS TO JUSTIFY;

ACCEPT FAILURE AND
IMMEDIATELY
RESTART YOUR
NEW SUCCESS JOURNEY...

www.SuccessCoachNilesh.com

" A mistake is simply another way of doing things. "

—Fkatherine Graham

Before you begin...

- **If you are:**
  - Not Happy with your Salary or
  - Not Happy with your Job or
  - Not Happy with your Career or
  - Working on the job that you don't like or
  - Working on the job that you don't want to do for the rest of your life or
  - Fed up or annoyed with your boss or
  - Aware that you can do better than your job colleagues or
  - Thinking about a business idea from the past few weeks or
  - Willing to establish your own business empire or

- Willing to receive more freedom and purpose in your life or
- Willing to make more money via doing Business

Then you are, at the right place and at the right time.

In this intensive book, I will give you those crucial strategies which will help you to achieve your dream of Switching from Job to Successful Entrepreneurship. You'll Progress Faster on this journey.

I feel sad, bad and helpless after seeing working professionals who are not happy in their jobs.

These people work really hard, devote most part of their life to their employers but at the end of the day; they are tired and not happy with their life.

There is no passion and purpose in their life. They are only going for the jobs they don't like any more, work with people that they don't like and follow a boss they seldom agree with.

For years I was looking for some compatible solution to help them.

After years worth of study and experience, it became clear to me that all those people who are stuck in their jobs and looking for change need to SWITCH from Job to Entrepreneurship. Entrepreneurship can be the healthy way forward. It can give them freedom, a sense of purpose and fulfillment and in most cases the best financial returns.

However, the journey of SWITCHING job to Successful entrepreneurship is not easy.

There are numerous challenges faced by these budding entrepreneurs. I've personally experienced most of these challenges before I became a Successful Author, International Speaker and Branding Expert.

To help you further, I managed to identify 4 EASY STEPS to SWITCH from Job to Successful Entrepreneurship. These steps are so easy to learn and follow that anyone can use them. You can learn these more in detail in this book. By using these steps, you'll be able to say Good Bye to your job and boss. You can live your dream life. I can't wait to go further and share them with you.

Let's get started.

"Failure is simply the opportunity to begin again, this time more intelligently."

—Henry Ford

> *If you don't drive your business, you will be driven out of business.*
>
> —B. C. Forbes

WHY are you not able to SWITCH now?

You might have thought about starting your business or dreamt about entrepreneurship or even taken some steps towards it however you are still not as successful as you want to be.

If you are not able to SWITCH from Job to Successful Entrepreneurship then there might be certain things holding you back. As if you are trying to accelerate and there are some unknown breaks holding your car back.

Let's figure them out.

- **Worry for your financial safety**

Starting a new venture can be a very turbulent task. Entrepreneurship always makes you feel worried about the uncertainty of success. This worry multiplies if you have dependents. There are a number of businesses that fail every day and there are many entrepreneurs who have nothing to show for months and years. The idea of giving up a steady monthly income to an uncertain business can bring jitters. Moreover, it takes a lot of courage to put your savings on the line so that you can follow your dream. You may have the fear that if you give up your job to something that is not certain you may regret it later. The thought of not being able to pay the bills and not having enough money to cover regular expenses and business expenses can bring nightmares. One of the greatest challenges of business is funding. To tackle this problem you may have to borrow funds externally or internally. These borrowed funds can give sleepless nights especially when you are unable to repay them. All these thoughts stop you from taking BIG steps for your own entrepreneurial journey. All these fears are absolutely valid and it is very human to be scared of being broke.

- **Not having Knowledge of the exact next steps**

You may have a dream of doing something big. But the basic question that arises in your mind is "How and where do I start?". You tend to visualize a lot but don't know exactly how to go about it. You don't know the EXACT next steps you will need to take to start your successful business venture. There is a weird fear of the unknown that keeps gripping your mind which ultimately holds you back from taking that big decision. You might have considered further management studies but still remain confused regarding the EXACT steps. You might do market research and get information from many people but are unsure about how to start. This leads to delay, procrastination, over-analyzing and a never ending phase of planning. Everything you have thought might be looking great on paper but you are not sure how its implementation is going to be. Nobody in this world is born knowing everything. So this fear of not knowing the next steps is natural and fine.

- **Lack of a rich business idea**

   The basic question that might come to your mind is "Whether my business idea is worth investing my time, effort and money on?" Moreover, the fear that you are inexperienced in the field you are trying to get into might be crossing your mind. Your idea might be vague and it is waiting for further market research or testing the market for its validity and usefulness. If your idea is not a novel one you might fear if it will be able to sustain the competition. On the other hand if it's an absolutely out of the box idea, you might fear it would be considered a crazy one. You might fear that the business idea on which you are trying to establish your business might be a complete failure. Unfortunately, we are living in the world where people tend to enjoy other people's failures. The fear that your idea would be mocked by others or wouldn't work is quite scary and it is absolutely valid to have that fear.

- **Lack of required confidence**

You may not be sure if you are capable of doing it. You lack the confidence or faith in your dream to start your business. You may feel that you don't have that drive to take up the challenges that the business may throw at you. You tend to underestimate your capability. The relation of confidence and fears is inversely proportional. The lesser the confidence the greater the fears would be. As it's said, "The more you stare into the dark, the more you can see someone staring back at you". Self-Confidence plays a huge role in your entrepreneurial journey. If you are not confident, you'll hold yourself back from taking the necessary further steps.

- **Lack of a success coach/mentor**

"A mentor is someone who sees more talent and ability within you, than you see in yourself, and helps bring it out of you." Doing business alone can be admirable but it would be the most faulty way of doing the business. Having a mentor by your side can amplify your confidence. On the other hand, not having a mentor can make you feel helpless and directionless. You might not know whom to look up to when you have innumerable doubts regarding your business. You might not have that guiding light that will enlighten your path and direct you towards your goal. With no mentor by your side you may make slow progress and the idea of not having a mentor especially in the time of adversity might add to your fears, lower your confidence and shake up your decision of venturing into business.

- **Fear of failure**

All fears sum up together to fear of failure. The idea of failure itself is quite dreadful. A series of 'what if' questions keep crowding your mind. What if I fail? What if I am broke? What if I disappoint my family? What if people mock me? What if my idea doesn't work? Your mind may constantly keep finding answers to these questions and the response that your mind gives is in the form of procrastination, over analysis, fear, futile waste of energy and worries. As it is said, stop thinking and start living. You never realise when your fears and worries occupy a major portion of your mind. In the process of being over-meticulous, you dread to take risks and prefer to maintain the status-quo. And staying in the comfort zone comes naturally to human beings. This sheer fear of failure stops you from taking any progressive step from time to time. It seems absolutely real. Moreover, when you don't have a tried and tested backup plan to resolve the issues you feel fear for, you feel unmotivated to move ahead.

- ## Non-supportive people around you

With every decision you take in life there may be ten other people who oppose your decision. There are as many opinions as there are number of people in this world. After all, everybody has the freedom to speak. Not everybody you meet in life will support the decision you make. In fact those who do will be in a number you can count on your fingers. The moment you disclose your interest in business there will be a series of stories that you will hear about how things didn't work for somebody and how that 'somebody' is regretting in life. All these stories might add to your pre-existing fears. And to be honest these non-supportive people might not always be outsiders. They could be people as close as your spouse, parents, siblings, parents-in-law or friends. It doesn't mean that their intention is bad. It's just that they are too protective of you and don't want you to face any failure in life. It is but natural on their part. But the words of caution coming from your loved ones make you revisit your decision and be super cautious. This in turn restricts you from moving ahead with your decision.

- ## Lack of clarity

Clarity is Power and the antonym of clarity is vagueness. This vagueness makes you weak, vulnerable and powerless. You might have an hazy picture of what you want to do but you might not have the detailing that is required to accomplish it.

The lone idea of doing the business is not sufficient to take the plunge. You might not know how business works, what business you want to be in, how big you want to do your business, who your customers are going to be, what skills are required to run a business successfully, how to manage the funds etc. With lack of knowledge and lack of clarity fear creeps into your mind. You might start doubting your decision and might think to yourself that you've been crazy to get into unknown territory. This lack of clarity makes you hesitant to take the decision.

- **Lack of BIG dreams**

  Dreams give direction to your imagination. A lack of BIG dreams fails to use this hidden potential of the imagination. You don't strive to achieve anything until and unless you have the dream to be something or achieve something. Dreams drive your goals. With no big dream you tend to be happy with the existing situation and there is no ambition in life. You tend to think small. Your actions become slow or very minimal and ultimately you achieve very little.

- **Fear to Leave Your Comfort Zone**

  Right now you may be earning a good living, you are set in your job and the money you are getting.

  You are comfortable with your social circle at office and outside, therefore it doesn't seem to be urgent to do something for entrepreneurship. You are so comfortable with your comfort zone that even if you dream about starting a business, there is no real need of it for you. Therefore you keep postponing the important actions you need to take to become a successful entrepreneur. You feel fear about the unknown future and you may feel guilty in the future about leaving your comfort zone and making your life worse than what it is now.

Each of us has a personal comfort zone. We are used to working within that zone. It's our safe place where we can stay happy most of the time. Fear of leaving the comfort zone is the fear of change. But one must not forget that the one thing that is constant in this world is change. Sometimes change is forced upon us and at other times you have to bring in the change. But to achieve greater heights you will have to get out and do things beyond your comfort zone and accept the change that it will bring with it. During your entrepreneurship journey and on many occasions you may encounter failure, as failure is an inevitable part of the journey and on each encounter with failure your mind may tell you to go back to your comfort zone. But what you need to remember is that greater success is beyond your comfort zone because "Life begins at the end of your comfort zone"-Neale Donald Walsch

OOO

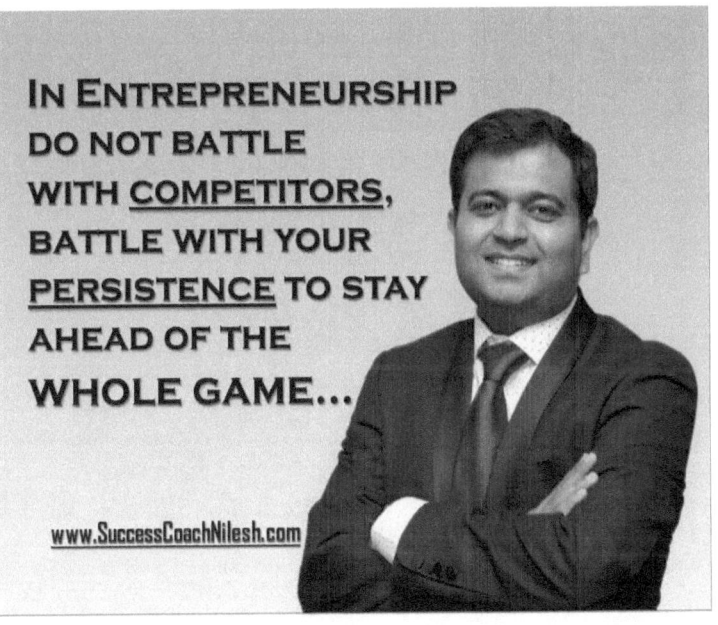

> "It takes 20 years to build a reputation and five minutes to ruin it. If you think about that, you'll do things differently."
>
> –Warren Buffett

WHAT do you need to SWITCH?

Once you figure out what is stopping you from the SWITCH, it's now time to find out what you need to SWITCH. What do you need to make your dreams come true, what should be your next step and how do you overcome your existing obstacles?

Let's find out.

- **Financial safety plan**

While you may say that to be a successful entrepreneur you need the right mind-set, you should not forget that you cannot ignore that one of the important aspects of business is 'cash'. You will be moving from a safe comfort zone to a not so safe comfort zone. As a salaried person you can expect a guaranteed pay cheque at the end of the month. But being an entrepreneur, you might not know when to expect that cash. So, before quitting your job you need to keep aside funds for your business. Apart from that you need to have enough savings to survive for about a year or so, as initially there could be some uncertainties in your business. As it is said "Money Grows by Management". If you start to manage money, doesn't matter how small an amount it is, then it's absolutely certain that you can grow it. On the other hand you can keep your full time job and start working part time for your business until your business stabilizes. Start generating profit at least as much as your monthly salary. Then work out a strategy to double your profits. Once you do that you would be in a better position to take that leap of faith for entrepreneurial success.

- **Knowledge of the exact next steps**

You must do your homework and get your facts right before you plunge into entrepreneurship. You need to have a passion for what you do and your passion needs to be aligned to the opportunity. You need to study the market and understand how your business would solve the problem that the market is facing. You need to know in and out about your target customers and their needs. You need to know your product or your service and the way it could tap the market. You need to have comprehensive market information, know the market trends and segmentation and perform a SWOT analysis before entering the market. Apart from this, you have to gain knowledge on business strategy, effective costing, quality and patenting your product so that you have an edge over your competitors. Gaining sufficient knowledge about fund management, marketing strategy, sales strategy and team building is also extremely essential. With this homework, you'll be in a better position to figure out your step by step plan to reach your ultimate business destination.

Don't worry for now. I'm going to cover this for you in the upcoming pages of this book. You are in good hands ☺.

- **A proven business idea**

Many people start a business and soon they realize that their business idea is not working. It is full of loopholes. So they choose to copy others. They think it is easy to copy as everyone else in the market is doing the same.

There is no harm in going the tried and tested way. But one should not forget that your product or service needs to have an edge over the others.

You need to determine why a customer would buy **your** product if there is a similar product in the market? In what way is your product better than your competitors? It could be in the aspect of price, quality or better discount offers.

The best way to do this is to perform a market analysis or survey. On the contrary if you have a completely unique idea, you need to check on its market saleability. Your product or service should be solving the customers pre-existing problem in an efficient way. You need to know if customers are ready to pay for your product or service repeatedly. Whatever your business idea, a market analysis is extremely important before going for it.

- **Confidence**

Being a successful entrepreneur is impossible if you lack confidence. You need to do all the research and be knowledgeable in your field before you start your new venture. Even when you face failure, you should be confident that you will turn that failure into success. You gain confidence if your passion is strong and you have complete faith in your idea. Moreover, getting the support of your loved ones would definitely add up to your confidence. Knowing that whatever the consequence may be, your loved ones would stay by your side gives you the required peace of mind. Apart from the emotional way, the more pragmatic approach could be including the necessary risk mitigation steps so that you don't have to worry in times of adversity.

- **Success coach or mentor**

You always feel secure under the assuring umbrella of a mentor. When you have doubts, fear, lack of confidence and lack of knowledge a reliable success coach can always help you

He can guide you about your next steps, give you the required motivation and assurance, help you resolve confidence issues, help you with tried and tested business strategies and make complex things easy for you. But good mentors don't just appear out of nowhere. To get a good mentor you need to keep your eyes and ears open. Mentoring can also happen online. Your mentor could be writing blogs. By reading his blogs you could learn a lot .You could also accept mentorship from someone who is already mentoring, coaching and helping others. This way you can get the required guidance at each and every step of your endeavour.

Check this out www.SuccessCoachNilesh.com for further Success Resources for you. Some of them are Free and some need investment. In any case, you'll love it.

• Strategies for success

Success does not just HAPPEN to anyone. Before starting your business, you have to do the necessary research in your field. You should learn not only the success stories but also failure stories of people who have previously done a business similar to yours. Remember "Failure is a much more faithful teacher than immediate success"-David Duchemin. By studying people's failed stories you would know what not to do. Apart from this, you need to listen to your customer's feedback and adapt accordingly, and be aware of the new market trends, products and services. You need to keep a close eye on your competitor's products and marketing strategies. Based on these you can make your own strategies to succeed!

• Supportive team

There's a well-known phrase "It's lonely at the top". But it would be foolish to think that great leaders reach the pinnacle of success without the help of an efficient team. You cannot run a business by yourself. You need a strong team behind you.

Behind every successful leader there is a team that supports, advices and works on the ideas that has originated from the entrepreneur's mind. During the initial phases of business an entrepreneur may find it comfortable to do things all alone. But as the company starts to grow, it becomes absolutely essential to delegate work so that you can concentrate on other important aspects of the business. But you should remember, every team member has unique strengths and weaknesses. Identifying the strengths and weaknesses of your team members and taking them along is the sign of a good leader. Once the team develops faith in their leader, they will put in all their efforts to make it happen. So "If you want to go fast, go alone. If you want to go far, go together"- African Proverb

• **Clarity of the future**

"Clarity is the most important thing. If you are not clear, nothing is going to happen. You have to be clear about your expected outcomes. Then you have to be confident about your vision. And after that, you just have to put a lot of work in"-Diane von Furstenberg.

Most entrepreneurs have some purpose before starting the business that makes them pursue their goal. But successful entrepreneurs develop a vision to take their business to greater heights. An aimless & directionless goal can take you nowhere. You should always have a clear idea about the expected future. You need to be clear about how big you want to make your business or where you want to take it.

Apart from this, you need to revisit your goal at every step to check if it's on track. Only when you are clear regarding where your business should be in the next 5 years, you will be able to direct your effort towards it. A well-directed vision acts as a source of self-motivation for you to keep moving ahead.

- **Big dreams and passion**

Have you ever dreamt of becoming the CEO of a company? Have you ever thought that your company is competing with the best companies in the world? Have you ever thought that your company could top the Forbes list? If your answer to any of these questions is yes... then indeed you have a big dream. Only when you picture what your dream is; you get the power to make it happen.

Big Dreams have hidden powers. They pull you towards them. There is a famous American saying "The Bigger the WHY the EASIER is the HOW". When your dreams are Big, you start to think Big. You start to think about BIG actions. You get motivated to take Big Actions and ultimately you achieve big things.

As you know, if you shoot for the moon, then even if you miss, you will land in stars.

Therefore always have Big Dreams. Big dreams give you a constant flow of motivation.

It helps you develop a steady focus on your goal without getting distracted. It makes you creative, passionate and pushes you forward to do the best possible thing to achieve your goal.

- **Effective blueprint to succeed**

As dreams and passions help you set a goal, an effective blue print helps you manage the steps to achieve that goal. An effective blueprint helps you to stay on your strategy, to prioritise, to understand the interdependencies between different tasks, to manage team members, to delegate tasks, to manage risks and uncertainties, to manage funds and cash flow, to track results and to correct the course of action if required.

Yes, you need an effective blueprint to succeed. You need to be clear about what direction to go in, the exact strategies, the correct ideas and a proper plan!

A Blueprint is the backbone of Great Achievements. Every famous monument had a blueprint before people made it. Your business is your monument. Make a blueprint to make it a success.

Don't worry for now. I'm also going to cover this for you in the upcoming pages of this book. You are in safe hands ☺.

> " I have not failed.
> I've just found 10,000
> ways that won't work. "
>
> – Thomas A. Edison

" *It's fine to celebrate success but it is more important to heed the lessons of failure.* "

– *Bill Gates*

Benefits if you SWITCH...

The Human mind is magical. All the decisions it makes are primarily guided by pain vs. pleasure feelings. We do certain things to avoid pain and we do certain things to seek pleasure.

The reasons to switch from Job to Successful Entrepreneurship, can be emotional. It will fluctuate between pain and pleasure feelings. To help you make a knowledgeable decision, here are the benefits of becoming an Entrepreneur.

- **Opportunity to change the world**

If you randomly catch hold of anybody and ask them regarding the change that is required in this world, you will find endless number of complaints about what's not right. In fact, it's always easy to sit and complain. What is hard is to bring about the change.

Entrepreneurship gives you the power to do exactly that. Being a successful entrepreneur is not always about making the most money. It's about getting a wonderful opportunity to make the positive change you want to see in this world.

Entrepreneurship and philanthropy go hand in hand. The passion to pursue the dream is the same drive that leads you to give back to the society. Helping others give entrepreneurs a sense of satisfaction and fulfilment that helps them cope with the daily stress of life. According to a study, 89% of entrepreneurs donate money for charitable causes and 71% donate their time. They believe that they are motivated to do more charity because they are entrepreneurs. Social entrepreneurs create organisations and collect funds to tackle a number of different causes. Every small step taken by the entrepreneur brings in a major positive change in the society.

"Great companies start because
the founder wants to change the world,
not make a fast buck"

-Guy Kawasaki

- ## The chance to improve people's lives

Although job creation is one of the most important contributions that entrepreneurs make to improve people's lives, it is certainly not the only one. If you focus your energy on creativity and innovation you could play a major role in changing people's lives.

When you initially start your business, you may hire just one or two employees. But as your company grows you can generate more jobs for people in your community. These jobs in turn help in improving the economy. When people are employed they tend to spend money on local business and that helps local businesses flourish. This in turn leads to forming good relations with suppliers and vendors.

The presence of new flourishing companies in turn encourages others to open up new businesses and create more employment. Being an entrepreneur you can also affect people's lives through the channel of philanthropy. Apart from this, entrepreneurship also gives you the freedom to innovate or create products that could change the lives of people for the better.

- ## Your financial freedom

Being an entrepreneur you can reap high profits. Yes, this is something everyone yearns for. Your company's profits could be linked to the decisions you take for your company. Owning a business can lead to accumulation of wealth which you could invest to expand your business or diversify. Many times people feel they are not getting compensated for the work they do in their jobs. Being an entrepreneur gives you the freedom to reap the benefits of all your hard work and decisions.

- ### A sense of purpose in your life

Entrepreneurship gives you freedom from all bondages. You can follow your heart and do things you believe in rather than reluctantly doing work for someone else.

By having your own business you become your own boss. You can do what you really want to do for yourself.

Only you are accountable for the decisions you make for your company whether they are good or bad. Being in such a situation will make you feel responsible for everything that you do. It's an opportunity to live life without being judged or having regrets. This will give a sense of purpose to your life.

- ### Source of an alternate income

Managing your job and business sounds very tricky. It's like sailing on two boats at once. But what one needs to see is that you can open up for yourself multiple sources of income. This alternate source of income gives you the required peace of mind and financial stability. Even during the times when one of your sources of income has been affected you'll have the relief that you have alternate sources of income. Moreover, if you find that your business is not flourishing, you'll have no regrets regarding leaving your job and putting your family at financial risk. On the other hand you'll have no repentance regarding not giving your passion or dream an opportunity. So it would definitely be a win-win situation.

- **High level of job satisfaction**

    Being a successful entrepreneur gives you that confidence that cannot be attained through any other means. The passion and determination to purse your dream, the independence to create your business and take decisions for your business, the courage to face challenges and the opportunity to handpick and develop your team gives you an immense sense of satisfaction and fulfilment. The acceptance you receive from people, your financial freedom, and the success you reach will all give you the highest level of job satisfaction. As it's said "When you find that job that causes you to be excited everyday-forget about the pay-with people you love, doing what you love, it doesn't get any better than that."-Warren Buffett.

- **Meeting amazing people**

    Running a successful business requires a lot of networking at every stage. As an entrepreneur, you get an opportunity to meet brilliant minds from around the world and different walks of life. You encounter amazing people in your team and through your businesses. Meeting such people can influence your personal life as well as career to a greater extent. As it's said "If you hang out with chickens you're going to cluck and if you hang out with eagles you're going to fly"-Steve Maraboli

- **Time to look after your family and health**

One of the attractive factors of being an entrepreneur is flexibility. It means you don't have to work according to a set schedule and you can manage your time according to your family priorities. To be honest, it may not be possible in the initial phases of the business but once you reach a certain satisfactory level in your business you will be much clearer about how to manage it by devoting optimum time. In this way you will have the time to look after your family and take care of your health.

- **Freedom to live life on your own terms**

Freedom to pursue your dreams, to work where you want and when you want is one of the most important benefits of being an entrepreneur. You won't feel like you are working as you will be living your dream. As it's said, "If you love what you do you'll never work a day in your life". By being successful, you also get the financial security and freedom to live life on your terms. You don't have to depend on anyone else.

• Self-development

Life is all about self-development. You learn something new every day! Being a successful entrepreneur gives you exposure to a wide variety of situations and challenges which will certainly help you to develop yourself. It's said "Diamonds are formed under pressure". Being an entrepreneur you get to meet amazing people, face difficult and challenging situations and manage teams. Apart from that you also go through lots of ups and downs in business which brings out the best version of yourself every day. Meeting new people also lets you see life from a different perspective and learn amazing things.

"To be Successful Entrepreneur is a Learn-able Skill"

—Success Coach Nilesh

66 *Innovation distinguishes
between a leader and
a follower.* 99

—Steve Jobs

HOW to SWITCH?

The decision to SWITCH can be overwhelming however I am here to share with you a 4 step process which has worked for me and many others to systematically SWITCH from Job to Successful Entrepreneurship.

Here it is...

The 4 Easy Steps to SWITCH

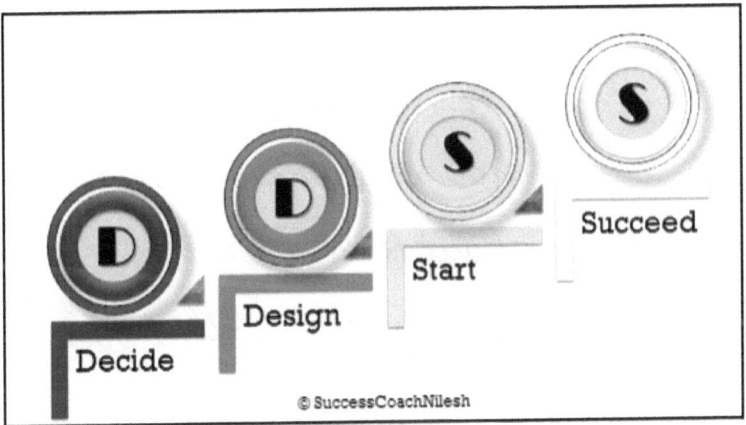

" *If you do build a great experience, customers tell each other about that. Word of mouth is very powerful.* "

– Jeff Bezos

" The cost of being wrong
is less than the cost
of doing nothing. "

–Seth Godin

DECIDE

Decide WHY you want to SWITCH.

Do you feel stuck in a regular 9-5 job? Or do you feel like you have no control over your life? Or that you are unable to do something innovative and worthwhile?

Or you feel like you want to give something back to the society and live your life according to your terms and conditions. Then the answer to all your questions is just one word, 'Entrepreneurship'. Yes, you heard it right. Entrepreneurship is like living a few years of your life like most people won't. So that you can spend the rest of your life like most people can't"-Anonymous

Life is always about choices. At every crossroad of life you need to make a choice about where you want to steer your life. So if your answer to one or more of the questions above is 'yes', then you need to definitely redirect your life towards the journey called Entrepreneurship. But a question may pop up into your mind about how Entrepreneurship can answer all your questions? Let me explain it to you in detail.

Most of you spend around 40 hours per week and sometimes more than that in a cubicle doing work which you have no ownership of, assigned by a manager who in turn works under somebody else. You come back home all drained out and at the end of the month you receive a pay check in lieu of all your hard work and loss of control over your life. Sometimes you even reluctantly work under somebody you don't like.

However, in Entrepreneurship it works the other way round. You are the boss or the owner. You call the shots and make the decisions for the company you own that can make or mar your business. You have complete authority over how things work in your company.

Entrepreneurship gives you the freedom to do things that are important to you and to chase your dreams. Each one of us is here on earth only for a stipulated period of time. This makes it very important that you make best use of the resources you have and achieve something worthwhile. Entrepreneurship lets you do exactly that. If you have any family or other circumstances that needs priority you can decide to forgo the work that day. Entrepreneurship gives you the flexibility to balance your work and family.

You get to make a big difference in the world with the ideas which might be considered unconventional by many. Entrepreneurship requires a lot of imagination and a dash of eccentricity. Entrepreneurs are the ones who make a big difference in the world. They want to see the world the way they want it to be and not how it presently is. From the brilliant ideas that made Steve Jobs build Apple or tech duo Larry Page and Sergey Brin invent Google, entrepreneurs pursue the dreams that others deem impossible.

You become the revenue generator and the jobs that your company generates become the source of livelihood and happiness for many. When you build up your dream business you get the golden opportunity to leave a legacy behind for the future generations. The business that started with your quest to prove your individual worth may become a business that may be cherished and nurtured by future generations long after you are gone. The company that was started by Henry Ford has passed through several generations and continues to create a major impact in the lives of many.

Have you ever had the fear of losing your job, getting laid off or being fired? Then you definitely know the value of job security. Entrepreneurship provides you job security as you are the owner of your company. So you never have to fear losing your job as you run the show.

Entrepreneurs are passionate about learning and they love to work with different people so that they can swap stories and learn from their experiences. Being an Entrepreneur, you get the chance to choose the people you want to work with and build a team from scratch and together achieve success.

So if you have decided to steer your life towards your passion of Entrepreneurship and have suitable reasons to pursue your passion then the time has come…and it is right now!! **"The critical ingredient is getting off your butt and doing something. It's as simple as that. A lot of people have ideas, but there are few who decide to do something about them now. Not tomorrow. Not next week. But today. The true entrepreneur is a doer, not a dreamer." –Nolan Bushnell, entrepreneur.**

Once you have decided why you want to be an Entrepreneur; you need to decide what you want to achieve as an Entrepreneur. Where you want to reach as a Successful Entrepreneur?

What business do you want to get into? Is it an online business or a physical shop selling useful stuff? Is it a product selling business or a services selling business or is it a beautiful combination? Do you want to create a local business or a global business? How much turnover are you aiming for?

Many people make choices based on the things they are good at. So if they work at a beauty salon they think of starting a business as a beautician or if they are a chef at a restaurant they think of starting a restaurant business all by themselves. Just because you are good at something doesn't mean you will be good at running that business.

Many others think of starting a business of things or product they love. Again, just because you love a product it doesn't automatically make you able to run a profitable business with that product.

You need to run a business of something that customers would love to buy or avail of not what you would love to sell. These are not the correct ways to choose your business. So, what is the right way to choose your business? To do that you need to find the answers to certain questions…

What product or service has a repeat value? Any product or service you sell or provide, people should be willing to come back repeatedly. That's what would make a business profitable. The number of times a customer comes back, that is how profitable the business would be. Additionally, it would create a stable customer base and positive word of mouth. This in turn would attract more customers.

Is there a specific type of customer you would love to sell your product or service to? It could be a customer of a specific age or income bracket. It could be a group of people with specific recreational interests or it could be people of a specific industry.

Is there a specific problem or need in the market and you can provide a solution to it? There could be a specific service or a product that customers would love to avail and you could provide them just that.

Is there a specific hobby or interest that could be turned into a business? You could have a hobby of knitting, dog breeding or designing beautiful pieces of jewelry. You can decide your target audience and focus on that.

How big do you want to make this as a business? Every big journey starts with small beginnings. But if you have a plan to take your venture to bigger heights you need to plan accordingly and create milestones so that you can tap your progress and check if things are working accordingly.

Do you want to run it locally or are you thinking about international business? You need to be sure about where you want to venture with your business. If it is a local business you need to identify your customers to whom you need to sell your product or provide your service or customers in the form of bigger firms to whom you sell your products or services. You also need to identify your local partners (if any) with whom you want to venture in with your business.

What are your thoughts on initial investment? You need to decide on how much you would like to invest in your business and shortlist the sources from where your business could be funded.

Many of you may think that it's easier said than done. But you need to start somewhere. You may have no knowledge about how to go about it, but this is how things start. Once you start, other things generally fall into place.

Steve Jobs –The Reed-College dropout started Apple Computers in his parent's garage. Mark Zuckerberg developed the social networking site 'Facebook' with friends while he was an undergrad at Harvard. Great things always start from small beginnings. Here's a beautiful quote from Mark Zuckerberg **"If you just work on stuff that you like and you're passionate about it, you don't have to have a master plan with how things will play out"**. Even if you fall or suffer a loss, you should be strong enough to face it and rise again. Don't be disappointed even if you fail in the first few attempts because every time you start again, you will be a wiser person with more experience that you gained from the last try.

After you decide your WHY and WHAT, the most important next step is **"Believe in your Dreams"**, even if you don't know the way forward. You should believe in yourself because you can build the faith, courage and enthusiasm within yourself for your success in business.

Remember that to be successful is a learnable skill. You can learn what you don't know, you can build networks, you can learn to market and you can learn to sell. Therefore dust yourself off and get up to get going with confidence.

Each one of you knows your strengths and weaknesses. You know what you want to achieve but the voice in you is dominated by your fears. One of the scariest moments is when you need to decide what business you should go for. Sometimes you kind of feel that it's a sheer lucky draw. Either you get to make a fortune or a pile of dung. But choosing business is not a random decision.

Make sure you believe in yourself because, Hey! if you won't then who else will? Making risky decisions takes a lot of courage and requires strong belief in oneself.

Last but not the least, make it happen by working for it. As Dr. APJ Abdul Kalam has said, "Dream is not what you see when you sleep, a dream is what does not let you sleep". Determination and strong will are vital for this step.

Always remember that as long as creating a positive difference in your life is the ultimate goal for you, trust me, when you become one of the leading entrepreneurs you will look back and smile. You will be proud of yourself and of your achievements.

Therefore DECIDE.

Summary—Decide Phase

Answer the questions below.

1) Why do you want to Switch from your exiting Job or Career?
2) Why do you want to become an Entrepreneur?
3) What difference do you want to create in this world and your life?
4) Where exactly do you want to REACH in your life/business?
5) When do you want all this to happen for you?
6) How will it feel when you become a successful entrepreneur?

"You will get all you want in life, if you help enough other people get what they want."

– Zig Ziglar

WHILE TAKING RISKS CALCULATE AND PROTECT YOUR LOSSES.

www.SuccessCoachNilesh.com

"The world is changing very fast. Big will not beat small anymore. It will be the fast beating the slow."

–Rupert Murdoch

DESIGN

Before you proceed with this section, make sure you have answered the 6 questions at the end of the DECIDE section.

Just like the rocket going into space needs fire at its bottom, an entrepreneur needs a reason to propel him/her forward to become a Successful Entrepreneur.

I hope you have a strong reason to move forward.

Well, let's move on.

Tell me, what is a Business?

Business is an Exchange. An exchange of value and money for a long period of time. You provide the value and your customers pay you in return. You provide value with the help of your products or services.

So far, you might have put yourself in a rapid fire round and tried to answer the questions to reduce your choices and decide on one business that you would like to do. But now, it's time for action.

Let's Design your next move.

First, Identify the problem in the market or the Opportunity to make something better. Then figure out your Solution to address that. Your Solution is your Product or Service.

You need to research to find the gap in the market. You need to meet people, search the net or observe your own family and friends to figure out what products or services are present in the market and what is lacking. With the help of this you could find the gap and your business could pitch in to fill the gap.

As I said previously that you need to sell a product or provide a service for which people should be ready to shell out their money repeatedly. To do this you need to tap the market to check if there is an existing product or service available in the market or not. If the answer is positive then you need to find out what is it that the existing product or service is lacking so that you can provide the improved version of the product or service that the customer would like to avail. A Cheaper or Better or Faster way is the solution.

The product or service could be tangible not only in quality but also in price. But in this process you need to know that you are doing a business and not social service. You need to make sure that you have a reasonable profit margin. There are very few companies that can compete in the long term with their "we are cheaper than them" marketing strategy.

Test your solution. Prove it's needed. Upgrade it if needed.

As you would test the depth of water before you dive in, you need to test your product or service before you launch because a business idea may sound great on paper but it may not work in reality. Sometimes your idea may be great but you may not have the skills to execute it.

To reduce the risk, observe someone in your prospective business. For example if you want to be a coach, observe someone who is already one; attend his seminars, observe how he provide solutions to people's problems. Then do an introspection and see if you see yourself doing that.

Other times a business succeeds due to extreme hard work and a huge investment. You need to be sure if you are ready to provide that amount of commitment and investment to bring your business dream into reality.

Before starting a business talk to people, friends, friends of friends and get their opinion and ask them to be brutally honest about your product or service. Offer them free samples of your product or service. Then take their feedback or testimonials to support you with your growth.

If you are providing a service or product, you need to ask potential clients and check if they are really willing to pay for your service. By testing the market you will not only gain confidence about your product or service but also test how you feel about it. If the product or service is accepted then proceed to go big. If the product or service is accepted with some feedback and comments then you need to upgrade it and retest it in the market. If the product or service is rejected then you need to change it. Don't give up. Just come up with a new product or service or combination which can be unique in the market. "If Plan A didn't work, the alphabet has 25 more letters! Stay cool"… Anonymous ☺

After successful completion of the test phase, you will feel a sense of satisfaction and purpose that will drive you forward.

Design success plans for your business. Make the Mission Accomplishment Plan (MAP) to go Big by collecting and managing the required resources.

You as an entrepreneur have a Mission. Your Mission is to create something valuable for the market and then exchange that for money.

Therefore you need a Mission Accomplishment Plan (MAP).

Imagine you want to go hiking in the forest. It is challenging, it is fun but it is also risky. To enjoy this adventure with satisfaction it is wise to have a map with you. It will help you plan your milestones and help you navigate.

Similarly, in Business you need a plan, a Mission Accomplishment Plan. All business experts agree on one thing and that is the importance of having a plan. Your plan is your list of milestones to achieve your business dream. Once you have this list, you can use it to navigate from milestone to milestone.

Many entrepreneurs avoid this crucial step. Plenty of them dive into the competitive arena of business without a formal plan. Why? Are you out of your mind? I've heard plenty of excuses over the last ten years.

A lot of new businesses are carried out thinking that their passion and optimism is enough to build a successful company. Others say they were just too busy to develop a formal business plan. But operating without a plan can prove even more time-consuming in the long run.

The benefits of having a Mission Accomplishment plan (Map) in Business:

The time you invest in creating your MAP will pay off many times over.

Some of the most obvious benefits you can gain from making this MAP include:

- Identifying where you are
- Identifying where you want to go
- Identifying your immediate possible milestones.

Apart from that, creating a MAP is:

- An opportunity to test out a new idea to see if it holds real promise of success
- A clear identification of your business mission and vision
- A set of ideas that can help you steer your business through times of trouble
- A blueprint you can use to focus your energy and keep your company and efforts on track
- A benchmark you can use to track your performance and make midcourse corrections
- A clear-eyed analysis of your industry, including opportunities and threats
- A detailed picture of your potential customers and their buying behaviors
- An inventory of your major competitors and your strategies for facing them
- An honest assessment of your company's strengths and weaknesses
- A roadmap and timetable for achieving your goals and objectives

- A description of the products and services you offer
- An explanation of your marketing strategies
- An analysis of your revenues, costs, and projected profits
- A description of your business model, or how you plan to make money and stay in business
- An action plan that anticipates potential detours or hurdles you may encounter
- A handbook for new employees describing who you are and what your company is all about
- A summary you can use to introduce your business to suppliers, vendors, lenders and others

What can go wrong without a plan?

The many benefits of having a business plan should be enough to convince you. But in case you're still wavering, consider what can go wrong if you don't take time to plan. You risk

- Running out of cash before you open your doors because you haven't anticipated your start-up costs
- Missing sales projections because you don't really know who your customers are and what they want

- Losing customers because your quality or service falls short
- Becoming overwhelmed by too many options because you never took the time to focus on a mission and vision for your company
- Going bankrupt because you don't have a rational business model or a plan for how to make money

Time spent putting together a solid Mission Accomplishment Plan for Business is time well spent. In fact, the more time you spend, the better prepared you'll be. But don't be overwhelmed at the prospect. The basic components of a Mission Accomplishment Plan for Business are moderately simple.

The 6 Key Elements of a Mission Accomplishment Plan for Business.

The good MAP will help you with the following:

1) To figure out where are you right now

2) To figure out where you want to go

3) To figure out your milestones

4) To figure out what you need along with you for your mission

5) To figure out what you need to prepare for, if things get worse than expected

6) To figure out how you can keep moving Forward

Let's identify the 6 Key elements of a Mission Accomplishment Plan

1) **Leadership:** The number # 1 reason why companies succeed or fail is its Leadership. Leader is the Driver behind the steering wheel of business. **You are the Leader in your business.**

   The perfect car can go in the wrong direction if the driver doesn't know where he is going.

   Great business leaders such as Steve Jobs, Bill Gates, Ratan Tata, Aziz Premji etc. have Vision for the future. They devote time, money and resources to do the right things whereas poor leaders spend time on getting things right.

2) **Market Study:** This will prove your knowledge about the particular industry your business is in. A market analysis forces the entrepreneur to become familiar with all aspects of the market so that the target market can be defined and the company can be positioned in order to collect its share of sales.

   A market analysis also enables the entrepreneur to establish pricing, distribution, sales and marketing strategies that will allow the company to become profitable within a competitive environment.

   In addition, it gives one an indication of the growth potential within the industry, and this will allow you to anticipate your own trends for the future.

Begin your market analysis by defining the market in terms of size, structure, growth prospects, trends and sales potential.

3) **Service and / or Product:** In business, entrepreneurs sell value in the form of a Product or Service or combination of them whereas customers buy a Product or Service or combination of them for obtaining the result they are aiming for.

What is it that you are actually selling? Make sure you emphasize the benefits (not the features). Establish your unique selling proposition. This means you have to show not only how your product is different but also why it is better.

4) **Marketing, Branding and Sales Strategies:** This is the lifeblood of your business. Marketing creates customers, Branding attracts and keeps the customers and customers generate sales. This will help you define your strategic plan to succeed in Marketing, Branding and Sales.

Remember that these strategies will be constantly upgraded based on your results.

5) **Team:** Build a strong support system because a mere idea won't fetch you anything. Many people start their business venture without any support. But you need to get a team of sales people, advisors, accountants and coaches to guide you at each step. Because a good team

will greatly improve your chances of launching a successful business.

If you are tight on budget then hire them on a part-time basis or get help from your friends and relatives.

6) **Money:** This is the fuel that runs your business.

Make sure you have enough. If you don't have it then you'll need to figure out where to get it from.

You can borrow from friends, family, bank or investors.

In this section, state the amount of funding you will need to start or expand your business. Include the best and worst case scenarios. Be realistic.

A good Mission Accomplishment Plan is never meant to be created once. And a good Entrepreneur understands that this MAP evolves as your business evolves and as your environment changes, as marketing campaigns exceed expectations or fail to meet your assumptions.

Re-visit your MAP weekly, monthly, quarterly and yearly.

Design your start point (The Launch day of your business)

After the planning is done you need to decide on the day you need to launch your product or service because unless a fixed date is decided you may try to procrastinate the launch due to fear of the unknown.

Launching a business needs a lot of preparation in the back-end. You need to create an efficient team who will be working for your business; you need a proper marketing strategy in place and finally you may also need to launch your website. Once everything is ready, you are ready to launch your business with a big bang.

Design your SWITCH point (E.g. Date and Year or Number or customers or Revenue Target or the Right Timing in the Market)

The whole idea why you are reading this book so far is to SWITCH from your current job/career to Entrepreneurship. Therefore you now have to think about that Exact SWITCH point.

Along with the launch date of your business you also need to set a date when you would completely switch over from your job to your business. Deciding this date is based on a target; a target that you set for your business. Your business target could be based on the number of customers you have to gain, target revenue your business has to achieve or profits you must make.

Ideally your switch date should be when your business breaks even and you now have enough funds in the bank to keep you afloat for at least 10-12 months.

Before switching completely from your job to your business you need to be dead-sure of your finances. Because once you leave your job your regular monthly income will come to a full stop and your business should be able to sustain you, your family and itself.

Financial Analysis for SWITCH Point.

The biggest roadblock people are facing is the financial security plan for their entrepreneurship journey.

But you don't have to worry about it now.

You can decide your switch point based on the following steps, which will help you take a calculated decision considering your financial situation.

Let's deal with it.

Take a pen and paper and do these calculations with me.

Remember where money is involved, numbers are involved and where numbers are involved calculations are needed. Calculations give them meaning.

Let's do those calculations.

1) Calculate your current monthly expenses (EMI payments, Light Bill, Newspaper bill, rent, grocery, children's fees, sundry expenses etc.)

2) Calculate your current yearly expenses (Car insurance, Car Servicing, Life Insurance, Annual trips, Children's school fees, Property Taxes etc.)

3) Calculate your combined expenses from step #1 and #2

4) What is your yearly NET (After Tax) income from all your current income sources (Salary, rent income, bank interest etc.)

5) What is Step # 4 – Step # 3?

6) Are you saving or losing money? (Positive amount for step # 5 means Saving and Negative amount for step # 5 means losing)

7) If you are saving, Good Job ☺, how much is that amount? If you are losing, ☹, how much is that amount?

8) If you are losing, please don't think about Entrepreneurship until you resolve your current money problems and until you have a positive outcome for step # 5.

Now, let's check your business side(Imagine you have now started your business).

9) What are your revenue and profit/Sales figures?

10) Are you making profit?

11) If not, how many more months would you need to generate profit and save money which equals your yearly expenses (as mentioned in Step# 3)?

12) If you are already making a decent profit then figure out how many more months you will need to save profits which will at least cover all your yearly expenses (as in Step # 3) ?

13) Calculate how long you can make that profit to avail a steady flow of income to cover all your expenses?

14) Based on the above calculations, figure out what the best time is for you to SWITCH?

15) Once you know the timeline in months, you can also figure out the date and year of the SWITCH.

Business does not always lead you to a bed of roses. Especially in the initial phase, your business could be fragile and its running could not be hunky-dory. So it would be wise that you set a stop point for your business. This stop point will decide the threshold level up to which you are ready to incur losses in your business.

Along with the **stop point** you need to have some risk mitigation steps in place. Risk mitigation would hold a very important part in your business forecast. It would give your business the required cushioning to sustain the initial bumpy ride. One of the Risk mitigation steps could be holding an insurance to protect your family and business in case of crisis. Some other steps could be to have surplus funds in hand so that your business can sail smoothly until it starts making profits.

Though business is an on-going process, it should not be vague. You need to have a definite goal or a destination to reach. Along with that you need to set up a timeframe and financial limit for your specific goal. This will work as a compass for your business that will guide you to achieve your destination. If by chance you think your business is not going the desired way you can trace back your steps and start again. Record your learning and keep a track of your business. This will help you in the long run.

- **Factor of Safety:**

Making a safety net is a sensible way to go. Always follow the prudence concept and build a safe side for every step you take. This step is important to be taken seriously because a business is always about playing with risks and if you acknowledge that, you should build a safety valve to be able to minimize the impact when the crisis hits.

E.g. Just be extra safe and multiply 1.5 as the factor of safety.

If you think your SWITCH point is 6 months away, make it 9 months by adding the factor of safety or if you think you need 50000 profit a month to make the switch make it 75000 to be extra safe.

Summary—Design Phase

Do the following things in the Design phase

1) Identify a problem in the market or an opportunity to make something better

2) Find the Gap in the market and create a solution to fill that gap. (E.g. A product or a service or a combination of a Product or Service)

3) Test your Solution. Prove it's needed. Upgrade it if needed.

4) Design your Launch.

5) Make a Mission Accomplishment Plan.

6) Design the Start Point.

7) Design the SWITCH point.

8) Design the STOP point as well.

9) Estimate the Time needed to reach SWITCH point.

10) Estimate the amount of money needed to reach SWITCH point.

11) Do a Financial Analysis

12) Add Factor of Safety.

> "You don't learn to walk by following rules. You learn by doing, and by falling over."
>
> – Richard Branson

WHEN YOU SEE **BIG** DREAMS AND WORK FOR THEM, IT ALSO INSPIRES; OTHERS.

www.SuccessCoachNilesh.com

> " *If you can dream it,*
> *you can do it.* "
>
> *–Walt Disney*

START

Once all the phases of DESIGN are done it's time to start the business. It's common and absolutely fine to feel the initial jitters. But you should remember that it should not hinder you from making progress.

There is a famous quote from Zig Ziglar:

"You don't have to be great to start, however you have to start to become great."

Businesses do not become successful overnight. It requires hard work, perseverance and the ability to take risk to achieve your dreams.

I know that you need to get together all the bits and pieces to build a business. You need to get your team in place, set an appropriate place for your office, make your product ready, do mega promotions for your product or service to attract your potential customers and provide appropriate promotional options to retain your customers.

Let me tell you two secrets.

A) "You don't have to do everything, NOW". You can do them one by one.

B) "You don't have to be perfect at everything at the beginning"

The Wish to be Perfect in everything is a trap. That keeps you away from the real entrepreneurship game.

If you really want to get going follow my 3 step rule – **Get in the Game, Stay in the Game and Grow in the Game.**

Once the business is on a roll, time management will play a very crucial role. It will be a juggle between business, job, family and you.

Good businessmen are excellent time managers. You need to divide your day and give sufficient time for your job, business, family and yourself. But you should know that since your business would be quite new you may have to focus more on it than others.

In such a situation you need to sit with your family and make them understand the need of the hour. By doing this you may get that required moral support to manage everything smoothly.

Ignoring your job too would not be a wise option as your job is the one that's bringing funds to sustain your family and your business to some extent.

In the process of managing everything successfully you must not forget your health as everything else makes sense only as far as your health is fine.

The wisest proposal would be to maintain a balanced act. So your timetable for the day could be something like this:

(1) **Job time:** This will help you earn the money and keep managing your existing expenses and save some money for your business. You can spare 7-10 hours a day for this.

(2) **Business time:** This will help you make progress on your business goals. You can spare 2-4 hours a day. It can be early morning or late nights.

(3) **Personal time:** This will help you unwind, relax and have some 'me' time. Sleep well but not too much. You can spare 6-7 hours a day for this.

(4) **Family time:** While you are working on your business, your family shouldn't get ignored. Make sure you inform them about your entrepreneurial efforts. Many times they may not agree with you or support you, however they will be aware of your time needs and at least they will support you there. Depending on your family you can spare 1-3hrs a day.

(5) **Health time:** If you are healthy only then can you make your business healthy. Therefore make sure you spare some time every day to

look after yourself. Look after what you eat and drink. Keep your body fit and functional. You can spare as little as 5 minutes per day but make sure you do it.

Here are some useful strategies to help you manage your time:

Strategy # 1:

Your time is constant but the tasks are not. Hence in reality you have to manage the tasks in hand not time.

Strategy # 2:

Mornings of any day are very useful and powerful. Hence decide your agenda for the day before you even actually start your work for the day. All the successful people use this technique. This gives power to your day. Hence instead of just passing through the day you will now start extracting results out of the day.

Strategy # 3:

Do more things that matter the most and do less things that matter less.

Strategy # 4:

Don't keep all your tasks in your head. Take it out. Put it on paper or the to-do list of your mobile phone. This leaves your mind free to think and this increases your mental power to deal with tasks.

Strategy # 5:

Always group your tasks as mentioned below:

Group A : Urgent as well as Important

Group B : Only Urgent

Group C : Only Important

Group D : All the others

You will notice, all of your tasks are not of equal importance. Hence group them appropriately so that you can deal with them in the order of required attention.

The recommended order of attention is Group A, then Group B, then Group C & then Group D.

Strategy # 6:

It's up to you how you wish to deal with different tasks. You may choose to do easy tasks first or difficult tasks first. Whatever you do doesn't matter as long as they are in the order of required attention.

Strategy # 7:

Many people think you cannot buy time but my friend, that's not true. You can buy time for yourself by hiring the services of others. E.g. Get your gardening done by professionals so that it will make time for you to take care of other important tasks.

Strategy # 8:

Do the Group A, Group B & Group C tasks in spite of your mood. Take some breaks, listen to music but do it.

All the successful people act in spite of their mood.

Strategy # 9:

Be realistic with yourself about how much you can actually accomplish in a given time. Don't over-pressurize yourself. Stay practical. Stay Real.

Strategy # 10:

You don't have to accomplish everything today. Set the tasks for the day, for the week, for the month, for the quarter, for six months, for the year etc.

Strategy # 11:

Expect interruptions, but come up with methods of dealing with them quickly and get back on track.

If you understand and use these strategies you will be successful in your life. Feel free to share these strategies with your friends, family and relatives.

The other essential thing to manage well along with time would be money. In the initial phases of the business money matters will be tight and grim. In such situations your job will be a ray of hope. Therefore while working on the job, make sure you save some funds which you can invest in your own business.

As a guideline:

Use 50-55% of funds for your expenses

Use 20-25% of funds for your business

Use 20-30% of funds for your savings

If your expenses are high, control them to keep it on track. Use your savings for business or personal emergencies. As I mentioned earlier, your risk mitigation steps would also mark an important step. A Great Business person knows the value of money and this is your chance to learn the skills to become a Great Business person.

Summary—Start Phase

1) START your Business

2) START Managing Your Time

3) START Managing Your Money

*Design is not just what
it looks like and feels like.
Design is how it works.*

–Steve Jobs

> " *As long as your going to be thinking anyway, think big.* "
>
> —Donald Trump

SUCCEED

The most difficult thing ever could be to balance on two boats. In your case the two boats are your job and business.

Anyone who is keen on being an entrepreneur would want to completely put their heart and soul into business without being worried about other things. But the problem is until the business is not stable, balancing between the two boats is mandatory. At the back of your mind a question might be haunting you "How can I accelerate to reach my switch point goals?".

These three points will help you create a successful business.

Team: Don't be a "Do it all alone" person. There are many things to look after while running the business. However you don't have to do everything all alone. Get someone to help you manage the workload. Delegate admin tasks to them which can free you up to do the main and most important things for your business. You might need to pay them salary however that will free you up to look after high value activities for your business.

Sales Strategy: Sales drive money into the business and when business has good cash flow it grows faster. Therefore the moment you have a working product/service which is adding value to your customers, start thinking about the sales strategy. You need to get answers to these questions... How to identify the target audience? How to get in touch with them? How to communicate your value to them and how to make an offer? Once you have all this in place it will make your life easy because you are being proactive and efficient.

System: Once you have a strategy and team in place, set up the systems. System is the process outline of how things will work in your business.

E.g. Who will do marketing, where will he/she check for customers, how will he approach them, how will he/she make an offer, who will look after the customers, the customer care, the delivery of the product, getting the testimonials etc. Once you have systems in place, it will make your life easy because you now have the business blueprint which works as designed.

"If you're walking down the right path and you're willing to keep walking, eventually you'll make progress." -Barack Obama.

At each and every step of your business it is extremely important to measure your progress and goals. That will help you stay focused and to know if your steps are well inclined to your ultimate goal. Moreover, each milestone achieved will give a sense of accomplishment and pride. It is said that, what gets measured gets done. Same is the case with your entrepreneurial goals. You are on the journey to reach your SWITCH point, therefore keep an eye on the measurable. It's like keeping an eye on the fuel level in your car.

Keep an eye on the amount of work you are getting done in the available time. Keep an eye on your income, savings and expenses to look after the business goals.

Keep an eye on how your product or service is behaving, how much revenue it is generating, is it as per your forecasts etc.

Finally, if you feel the day has arrived and your business is stable then that would be the day of your complete switch over. Your journey so far would have been exhilarating.

You might have been through acute pressure and lots of stress. You might have been through a sense of joy and purpose.

You have been measuring your progress all along. Now, it makes perfect sense to go full time with the business.

You might feel that there is a lot of risk involved. But as it's said by Mark Zuckerberg **"The biggest risk is not taking any risk. In a world that is changing quickly, the only strategy that is guaranteed to fail is not taking any risk"**.

Moreover, this is a **calculated risk** and your past results have proven that it works. The fear you may be feeling is normal. It happens to all of us. Remember, there is success ahead of fears.

Therefore just do it.

As life has ups and downs your business too will have its share of ups and downs and that's what will make your business and yourself stronger. Each difficulty that will cross your path will teach you something that will help you in the long run. Some of the problems your business might face are abnormal loss, competitors, fall in demand and unpredicted loss. But you need to understand that these problems are a part of business life. In such situations the most important thing would be to keep calm and stay focused. Secondly, you need to analyze the different possible solutions to come out of such situations. The third step would be to compare all the solutions and then to choose and execute the best solution. Additionally, the risk mitigation steps would come in handy in case of adversity.

Business is not a one time investment. Here, by investment I don't mean just money but also effort and strategy. You need to keep refueling your business with better ideas and strategy to stay ahead in the game of business. The marketing strategy you have decided earlier may not work in the first attempt, the sales plan you have may not deliver results as expected, your team may not produce the output as expected however that's how the journey to success is for everyone. Every successful entrepreneur has gone through this. Do you think Bill Gates knew everything about his big plans for Microsoft or Steve jobs knew everything about the mobile and electronic market?

No way. They all learned through mistakes. They all learned from experiences. The only thing which made them great was that they kept improving their approach.

Whenever they came across obstacles, they worked to find the solution and they kept moving forward. That's what you should do too. Keep Moving Forward.

If you don't know something; learn it. If you don't have something; get it. Whatever happens keep moving forward, because that's what successful entrepreneurs do...

The things you regret most in life are the risks that you didn't take; But in your case it would be the opposite. Your life would have no regrets because you would have had the guts and the passion to chase your dream to become an entrepreneur. When you look back at your life you'll see passion, hardships, failures, trials and tribulations. But from the place where you would be standing it would all be worth it. All your hard work will start paying off as soon as you decide to bring a change and work for it. If you have followed every step then probably you're already here.

Congratulations friend! You've earned it.

Even if you haven't started and you are reading this then know that living your dream can actually become your reality. It's not too late for that.

"It always seems impossible until it's done"- Nelson Mandela.

All you have to do is make a decision and gather the courage to go in the direction of your dreams. This is the ultimate guide for that. All the Best!

In summary, to SUCCEED in your adventure:

1) Figure out how to accelerate your journey towards your SWITCH point

2) Get your Team, Sales Strategy and Systems in place.

3) Take help from your friends, families, relatives or ask me ☺. I'll be happy to help.

4) Measure your progress and compare it with your Switch point targets.

5) Reach your SWITCH point.

6) Just SWITCH it. Say Good bye to your Job and your boss. Shift Full time to Business.

7) Manage start-up difficulties, Stabilize and Grow.

8) Keep Moving Forward.

9) Congratulations ☺ You are already there!. Congratulations on your Great Achievement.

" *Never give up. Today is hard, tomorrow will be worse, but the day after tomorrow will be sunshine.* "

— Jack MA

17 ways to save money in your startup business

Running a start-up business can be quite challenging due to limited resources, especially finance. Using some innovative tips and tricks to handle finance and utilizing inexpensive ways to attract customers can save a major chunk of money. Here are some of the money tips that will help you utilize that shoestring budget effectively.

1. Handle your Marketing and PR on your own:

You can learn everything about your Marketing and PR strategy and handle the marketing of your product or service on your own and be the face and promoter of your product. As it's said, "You can't sell anything if you can't tell anything."-Beth Comstock. Hiring a PR team can be quite taxing for your budget so you can handle it by doing it yourself. Try innovative and creative marketing techniques. If things don't work that way, don't be hesitant to ask.

2.   Get help from a contented customer:

If you have a customer who is happy about your product or service, request for a testimonial from them which you could publish on your website or office display. You can provide the example of that customer in your business circle and also during presentations. Additionally, positive word of mouth from the contented customer can provide the added benefit for your business.

3.   Get help from people you know:

Be more vocal about your product in your friend and business circle. Request them to publicize your product in their circle. The more people become aware of your product the more business it will fetch you.

4.   Try to find sponsors for your promotional activities:

You can ask for sponsorship from existing big businesses in the market who might want to get promoted to your customers. The reason they will be happy to help you is that it can make their life easy & profitable as you get them in contact with your customers.

5.   Reduce your inventory expenses:

You can save quite a lot of money if you minimize your inventory expenses. You can make use of 'used' furniture, recycled cartridges, copiers and computer equipment.

6.   Provide expert advice:

You can write blogs or articles on Google+, Word press and Pinterest or give seminars and presentations to a group of people which would give you the much needed publicity and also increase your credibility.

7.   Try using free promotional avenues:

If you want people to know about your website or a blog, you can mention it over your letterhead, business card as well as in your e-mail signature. Additionally you can include it on your office vehicle or work uniform. This would help you get free publicity and awareness.

8.   Reduce the cost on your online store, if any:

If you are selling something online, then to start with, you can use pre-existing online stores such as Amazon, E-bay etc. If you are planning to set up your own exclusive store then it might be expensive at the beginning, this is also the case if you are not sure which are your best selling products.

9.   Hire able employees with less work experience:

If you hire people with entry level experience, they will be ready to work at entry level salaries. Additionally, able recruits with minimal experience require that needed break to prove themselves due to which they are much more eager to work well.

10.   Hire employees as per work load flow:

Instead of hiring full time employees, hire temporary employees who will work only when the business work load is more.

11.   Plan your payments:

Negotiate with your suppliers if you can pay later and negotiate with your customers if they are willing to pay earlier. It may not work for all kinds of businesses, however, it is worth trying.

12.   Become a member of a trade or business association:

Many business and trade associations have minimal membership fees. E.g. Chambers of Commerce. Trade associations can give access to innovative business strategies and practices. Being a member of such associations can improve your reputation and help you make more connections.

13.   Get advice from your consultant:

You can get advice from your CA, consultant or attorney about ways to save money on your premiums or other expenses. They can surely provide you help with great ideas on legal ways to optimize your tax.

14.   Be precautious about hidden costs:

When you hire a Supplier or website developer, make sure you have a proper written agreement. Read the clauses of the agreement thoroughly and be sure of the break-down of the fees so that there are no hidden additional fees.

15.   Take advantage of early deposits:

Make deposits early in the day so that you can start earning interest on that amount from the same day.

16.   Avoid giving credits:

Be reluctant on giving credit to your clients. But if you are in a situation where you have to give credit, be sure you check your client's credit history. Collect cash in advance or provide partial delivery until the payment is done.

17. Be insured:

Getting insured can save a lot of money in the long run. Be prepared for situations that can harm your business and yourself. No business owner should be thrifty on this one. For example: building or content insurance.

OOO

EVERY "FAILURE" CAN TAKE
YOU CLOSER TO
"SUCCESS". LEARN
THE LESSON AND JUST
KEEP MOVING FORWARD.

www.SuccessCoachNilesh.com

" Your time is limited, so don't waste it living someone else's life. "

— Steve Jobs

Before Saying Goodbye

Well done my Friend. I am sure you now have useful insights, strategies, plans and motivation to take the next steps, to start and grow your successful business. By the way, if you still have any doubts about failure, you have to read this.

Have you ever failed in life? If your answer is 'no' then unfortunately you have not tried enough because Failure is very much a part of Success. With every failed attempt you move a step away from your imperfections and move a step closer to wisdom and success.

Leaders always lead the way through example. Even the greatest of leaders like Steve Jobs had to face innumerable failed attempts. But what kept him moving was his unquenchable thirst for excellence and his tireless efforts. Look around you!! Even the tiniest of creatures like spiders will encourage you to keep trying and not giving up. This also inspired the great King Bruce to fight back and not give up. If you want to succeed you should be willing to fail and learn from your mistakes.

Remember: Never fear failure... The day of your failure will not be a day to grieve but a day to rejoice that you have crossed one more bridge and are moving closer to your goal to success and the day of getting ready to face your next upcoming challenge. So keep moving forward. You never know when success comes knocking at your door....Knock Knock!!!

All the Best.

Yours Truly,

Success Coach Nilesh

ABOUT THE AUTHOR...

Nilesh Waghchoude (also known as Success Coach Nilesh) is the best-selling Author, International Speaker and creator of Accelerated Success Techniques ® and Career Accelerator Roadmap®.

He has spoken at London Youth Conference, London Business School, Bradford School of Management, College of Engineering Pune- COEP, YASHADA Pune, Lila Poonawala Foundation, Maharashtra Mandal London, Junior Chamber International, UK etc.

He has also travelled and spoken in many countries around the world.

He has coached and consulted CEOs, Directors, Managers, Students, Entrepreneurs etc.

However, he started from the very bottom. Nilesh was born and brought up in India where English was not even his first language. After Studying at village and *Taluka* levels, he moved to Pune (One of the big cities in India) to study engineering. He was overwhelmed by the people and life in the city because he had never experienced that before. He had a lack of self-confidence, had self-doubt and negative beliefs. He even failed in his first year engineering exams. However, he kept going and graduated in engineering with a first class plus distinction.

Nilesh started his professional career as a Car Design Engineer. After working in India for a couple of years he went to the USA to work for his company's clients.

His professional career was great but he wanted to pursue his dream of completing an MBA. To achieve his dream, he quit his job and went to the United Kingdom for his Business studies.

After completing his MBA, he got an offer to work for one of the most prestigious luxury car companies in the UK and he started his job. He was very happy with his job, but this happiness didn't last long. Something was going to happen which would transform his life forever.

Due to the economic recession, his company undertook the lay-offs route. As Nilesh was fairly new in his job; he was amongst the people who got laid off.

This was a massive setback for Nilesh. He had a huge education loan to pay back and there were no signs of the economy recovering. He applied for thousands of jobs and what he got was only rejections.

Nothing seemed to be working for him. Nilesh began to think: How did he get here? How can he come out of this mess, survive and be successful?

At that moment he made a decision to change his bad situation and work diligently to become successful in his career.

He then started working part time for a very low paying job at the Arts Centre where his job was to check the tickets at the door of the venue.

During this time Nilesh also started his own Business consulting company. He realized that **'It's not our circumstances but our decisions that shape our lives & our future'.**

In his free time he started reading self-development books and listening to audio programs. He even attended LIVE training sessions, seminars and workshops by world-class people such as Tony Robbins, Les Brown, Harv Eker, Richard Branson, Donald Trump, Robert Kiyosaki, Brain Tracy etc. and his life started to get back on track.

Nilesh's perseverance resulted in him starting to deliver successful coaching and training sessions that transformed the lives of many individuals and businesses.

During the first year of the company he was a finalist for two prestigious awards by the Institute of Business Consulting UK.

(Best Newcomer to Consulting and Most Outstanding Achievement towards Continuous Professional Development)

Nilesh now takes Trainings, Consulting and one to one coaching sessions.

Nilesh teaches those Precise, Proven and Powerful Tools & Strategies which will help you make FASTER Progress in your Career, Business and Life.

Using the principles he now teaches, Nilesh has transformed his own life, career, finances, health, and relationships.

He now works with professionals from all over the world to provide them smart strategies to make faster progress in their lives & businesses.

These strategies are made up of several critical secrets absolutely necessary for **rapid & sustainable** personal, professional and business success.

So please don't even think of missing the information revealed in his books and sessions.

For further details on his sessions, trainings & workshops please visit:

www.SuccessCoachNilesh.com

So far Nilesh has helped his clients in following areas:

- ✓ Increasing their Income by 40-300% by his Efficient Money Management System (EMMS)

- ✓ Improving their Leadership, Communication, Public Speaking and Time Management skills to achieve Maximum Influence and Results in shorter time

- ✓ Developing Powerful Action Plans to Become More Efficient and Productive

- ✓ Building their own Businesses from Concept to Reality (C2R) in less than 30 days

- ✓ Feeling Confident at the Work place and Achieving Maximum Results

- ✓ Getting freedom from Fears and Stress

- ✓ Increasing their Savings by 20-50% by his Strategic Financial Planning (SFP)

- ✓ Achieving their Personal Goals and Becoming Successful Strategically & Quickly

- ✓ Developing Marketing & Sales Strategies which will work in real life to achieve Business Turnaround & Long Lasting Growth

- ✓ Becoming an Expert to make Faster Progress in their Career and Life

- ✓ Gaining Confidence & Power during Interviews.

- ✓ Designing a Personal Blueprint for Long-term Success

- ✓ And Many More topics to suit his clients' Special Needs

Other
Useful
Success Resources
for You
From

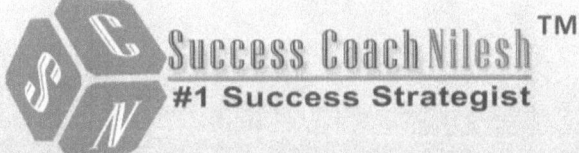

Quit Job. START Business.

Meet Nilesh @ . . .

❑ **Google:**
  Success Coach Nilesh

❑ **Linked In:**
  Success Coach Nilesh

❑ **Facebook:**
  ✓ Nilesh Waghchoude
  ✓ Success Coach Nilesh
  (Join our growing fan page)

❑ **You Tube:**
  Success Coach Nilesh

❑ **Slide Share:**
  Success Coach Nilesh

❑ **Twitter:**
  SuccessCNilesh

❑ **Instagram:**
  Success Coach Nilesh

❑ **Email:**
  MySuccess@SuccessCoachNilesh.com

Contact Nilesh @
www.SuccessCoachNilesh.com
Transform **Your** Life & **Business** in Next 30 **Days!**